Goldilock and the Three Bears

Retold by Barbara Mitchelhill
Illustrated by Michelle Mathers

Collins

C000005173

2

🐾 Ideas for guided reading 🐾

Learning objectives: understanding how story-book language works; using knowledge of familiar texts to re-enact or retell to others; learning new words from reading and shared experiences; exploring the sound effects of the story using instruments in a retelling; exploring familiar themes and characters through role-play.

Curriculum links: Communication, language and literacy: respond to and make up own stories; retell narratives in the correct sequence; mathematical development: use language of comparisons

Interest words: Goldilocks, three, bears

Getting started

- Tell the children that this story is about a little girl who has an adventure (keep the book hidden). Hot-seat as Goldilocks and ask the children to play 'Who am I?' by giving clues, e.g. I have long golden curls and I like porridge. Use interesting words, e.g. *angry, tired, hungry.* Prompt the children to ask questions such as 'Did you break Baby Bear's chair?'

- Show the book to the children and read the title together, pointing to each word in turn. Discuss what is happening in the cover picture.

- Ask the children what they already know about the story. What happens at the beginning, in the middle and at the end? Walk through the story together and discuss whether the story unfolds as they expect.

Reading and responding

- Ask the children to 'read' the story up to p13, prompting them to look carefully at the pictures and describe and explain what is happening. They should also look for and comment on any extra detail. Encourage them to use interesting words to describe things and feelings, e.g. 'lumpy porridge', 'angry bears'.

- Encourage the children to use sequencing language when discussing the sets of three pictures, e.g. 'first', 'then', 'next'.